MY LUCKY DAY

Keiko Kasza

PUFFIN BOOKS

For Hiroki

PUFFIN BOOKS
Published by the Penguin Group
Penguin Young Readers Group, 345 Hudson Street, New York, New York 10014, U.S.A.
Penguin Group (Canada), 10 Alcorn Avenue, Toronto, Ontario, Canada M4V 3B2
(a division of Pearson Penguin Canada Inc.)
Penguin Books Ltd, 80 Strand, London WC2R 0RL, England
Penguin Ireland, 25 St Stephen's Green, Dublin 2, Ireland
(a division of Penguin Books Ltd)
Penguin Group (Australia), 250 Camberwell Road, Camberwell, Victoria 3124, Australia
(a division of Pearson Australia Group Pty Ltd)
Penguin Books India Pvt Ltd, 11 Community Centre, Panchsheel Park, New Delhi - 110 017, India
Penguin Group (NZ), Cnr Airborne and Rosedale Roads, Albany, Auckland 1310, New Zealand
(a division of Pearson New Zealand Ltd)
Penguin Books (South Africa) (Pty) Ltd, 24 Sturdee Avenue, Rosebank, Johannesburg 2196, South Africa

Registered Offices: Penguin Books Ltd, 80 Strand, London WC2R 0RL, England

First published in the United States of America by G. P. Putnam's Sons,
a division of Penguin Young Readers Group, 2003
Published by Puffin Books, a division of Penguin Young Readers Group, 2005

1 3 5 7 9 10 8 6 4 2

THE LIBRARY OF CONGRESS HAS CATALOGED THE G. P. PUTNAM'S SONS EDITION AS FOLLOWS:
Kasza, Keiko.
My lucky day / Keiko Kasza.
p.   cm.
Summary: When a young pig knocks on a fox's door,
the fox thinks dinner has arrived, but the pig has other plans.
[1. Pigs—Fiction. 2. Foxes—Fiction.]
I. Title.   PZ7.K15645   My 2003   [E]—dc21   2001057874   ISBN: 0-399-23874-3 (hc)

Puffin Books ISBN 0-14-240456-X

Manufactured in China

One day, a hungry fox was preparing to hunt for his dinner. As he polished his claws, he was startled by a knock at the door.

"Hey, Rabbit!" someone yelled outside. "Are you home?"

Rabbit? thought the fox. *If there were any rabbits in here, I'd have eaten them for breakfast.*

When the fox opened the door, there stood a delicious-looking piglet.

"Oh, no!" screamed the piglet.

"Oh, yes!" cried the fox. "You've come to the right place."

He grabbed the piglet and hauled him inside.

"This must be my lucky day!" the fox shouted.
"How often does dinner come knocking on the
door?"

The piglet kicked and squealed, "Let me go! Let
me go!"

"Sorry, pal," said the fox. "This isn't just any
dinner. It's a pig roast. My favorite! Now get into
this roasting pan."

It was useless to struggle. "All right," sighed the piglet. "I will. But there is just one thing."

"What?" growled the fox.

"Well, I am a pig, you know. I'm filthy. Shouldn't you wash me first? Just a thought, Mr. Fox."

"Hmmm . . ." the fox said to himself, "he is filthy."

So the fox got busy.

He collected twigs.

He made a fire.

He carried in the water.

And, finally, he gave the piglet a nice bath.
"You're a terrific scrubber," said the piglet.

"There," said the fox. "Now you're the cleanest piglet in the county. You stay still, now!"

"All right," sighed the piglet. "I will. But . . ."

"But what?" growled the fox.

"Well, I am a very small piglet, you know. Shouldn't you fatten me up to get more meat? Just a thought, Mr. Fox."

"Hmmm . . ." the fox said to himself, "he is on the small side."

So the fox got busy.

He picked tomatoes.

He made spaghetti.

He baked cookies.

And, finally, he gave the piglet a nice dinner.
"You're a terrific cook," said the piglet.

"There," said the fox. "Now you're the fattest piglet in the county. So get into the oven!"

"All right," sighed the piglet. "I will. But . . ."

"What? What? WHAT?" shouted the fox.

"Well, I am a hardworking pig, you know. My meat is awfully tough. Shouldn't you massage me first to make a more tender roast? Just a thought, Mr. Fox."

"Hmmm . . ." the fox said to himself, "I do prefer tender meat."

So the fox got busy.

He pushed . . .

and he pulled.

He squeezed and he pounded the piglet from head to toe.
"You give a terrific massage," said the piglet.

"But," the piglet continued, "I've been working really hard lately. My back is awfully stiff. Could you push a bit harder, Mr. Fox? A little to the right, please . . . yes, yes . . . now just a little to the left . . .

"Mr. Fox, are you there?"

But Mr. Fox was no longer listening. He had passed out, exhausted. He couldn't lift a finger, let alone a roasting pan.

"Poor Mr. Fox," sighed the piglet. "He's had a busy day." Then the cleanest, fattest and softest piglet in the county picked up the rest of his cookies and headed for home.

"What a bath! What a dinner! What a massage!"
cried the piglet. "This must be my lucky day!"

When he got home, the piglet relaxed before a warm fire. "Let's see," he wondered, looking at his address book. "Who shall I visit next?"

Fox
Log Cabin up on the hill

Wolf
Next to the tallest pine tree

Bear
House with red roof by the river

Coyote
Cave under the hanging rock